J
E

Partridge, Eliza-
beth

Annie and Bo and
the big surprise

Annie and Bo and the BIG SURPRISE

BY **Elizabeth Partridge**

ILLUSTRATED BY **Martha Weston**

DUTTON CHILDREN'S BOOKS • NEW YORK

Library of Congress Cataloging-in-Publication Data
Partridge, Elizabeth.
Annie and Bo and the big surprise / by Elizabeth Partridge;
illustrated by Martha Weston—1st ed.   p. cm.
Summary: Bo bakes a full moon cake as a surprise
for his friend Annie, but the outcome is unexpected.
ISBN 0-525-46728-9
[1. Cake—Fiction. 2. Baking—Fiction. 3. Mice—Fiction.]
1.Weston, Martha, ill. II. Title. PZ7.P26 An 2001 [E]—dc21 00-065432

Published in the United States 2001 by Dutton Children's Books,
a division of Penguin Putnam Books for Young Readers
345 Hudson Street, New York, New York 10014
www.penguinputnam.com

Designed by Sara Reynolds
Printed in China   First Edition
1 3 5 7 9 10 8 6 4 2

To the newest Ratlets:
Georgia, Abby, and Pommy

E.P.

To Marrie,
wonderful sister, wonderful friend

M.W.

Bo could not sleep.

Tomorrow he was going skating.

He was going

with his best friend, Annie.

He wanted to give Annie a surprise.

A wonderful, big surprise.

But what?

After all, she was his best friend

in the whole world.

Bo jumped out of bed.

Maybe Annie would like his new drawing.

Maybe not.

Annie did not like scary things.

Bo looked in his bag of marbles.

Maybe Annie would like one.

But he might need all of them.

Bo looked under his bed.

What about his yellow tail sock?

But then his tail would get cold.

Bo stared out the window.

He couldn't think of anything

to give Annie.

He saw the full moon shining

on the snow.

"Oh, moon!" Bo said.

"You are so big and

round and golden.

Now I know what to do.

Tomorrow I will give Annie the moon."

Bo woke up early.

He ran downstairs to the kitchen.

He worked hard.

He worked fast.

He made a big mess.

There was flour in his fur.

There were eggshells in the sink.

Batter flew all around.

Bo didn't care.

He poured the batter into a pan.

"I will call this

a full moon cake," he said.

He picked up the pan and danced around.

"You are big.

You are round.

You are golden.

You will be a perfect surprise for Annie!"

Bo put the pan in the oven

and set the timer.

Then he sat down to wait.

Tick, tick, tick...

CHAPTER 3

Annie jumped out of bed.

She dressed quickly.

She put on her coat.

She put on her mittens.

She put on her warm tail sock.

She grabbed her skates

and ran over to Bo's house.

Thump, thump, thump!

Annie knocked on Bo's door.

"Bo! It's me!" she called.

Bo knew that voice.

It was Annie.

He ran to the door.

Just then the timer went off. *Ding!*

The cake was done.

Bo ran back to the kitchen.

Annie could hear Bo running around.

"What are you doing?" called Annie.

"Open the door. I'm freezing."

Bo pulled the cake out of the oven.

He ran back to the door.

"Let me in!" said Annie.

"Soon I will be frozen stiff."

Bo did not want Annie to see

the surprise.

He did not want her to smell

the surprise.

"You can't come in!" yelled Bo.

"I will come out in a minute."

CHAPTER 4

Bo ran out and slammed the door

behind him.

He smiled at Annie.

It was a great big smile.

It was a fake smile.

Bo couldn't fool his best friend.

"Bo," said Annie. "What are you hiding?"

"Annie," he said. "I am

making you a surprise.

You can't come inside."

"A surprise?" said Annie. "For me?"

She threw her arms around him.

"Ouff!" said Bo.

"What is it?" she asked.

"If I told you, it would not be a surprise,"

said Bo.

"Anyway, it's not ready yet.

 Let's go skating."

"Okay. But there is just one thing,"

 said Annie.

"What?" asked Bo.

"You better get dressed first," she said.

Annie and Bo skated for a long time.

Bo skated fast.

He did high jumps and spins.

He felt the wind in his whiskers.

He heard the *shush-shush-shush*

of his skates on the ice.

Annie skated slow.

She didn't feel the wind in her whiskers.

She didn't hear the *shush-shush-shush*

of her skates on the ice.

She was wondering about her surprise.

"Is my surprise big?" she asked.

"Bigger than what?" said Bo.

"Bigger than me," Annie said.

"No," said Bo. "It's not bigger than you."

"Too bad," said Annie. "I like big

surprises."

"In fact," said Bo, "the surprise will

fit inside you!"

"That is a very small surprise," said Annie.

"Don't worry," said Bo.

"It's small enough to fit inside you,

but it's also big."

"Quit teasing me!" said Annie.

"I'm not teasing you," said Bo.

He could not wait any longer.

He wanted to give Annie her surprise.

"I have to go home now," he said.

"I will come to your house later."

"With the surprise?" asked Annie.

"You'll see!" said Bo.

Annie got ready for Bo.

She made two bowls of carrot soup.

Bo loved carrot soup.

But Bo didn't come.

Annie ate her bowl of soup alone.

Maybe Bo forgot, Annie thought.

Maybe he changed his mind.

Maybe he was going to keep the surprise.

Annie sucked on her tail and worried.

Bo had not forgotten.

He had not changed his mind.

He was working hard.

He was making a bigger mess.

Bo didn't care.

He was frosting the full moon cake.

31

Annie saw the moon come up.

She worried some more.

Maybe Bo was lost in the dark.

Maybe he had slipped and fallen.

Maybe he was alone in the snow.

Bo was not lost.

He was still at home.

He was looking for a big box.

He found the perfect one.

He put the cake inside the box

and took off for Annie's.

Annie could not wait any longer.

She put on her coat.

She put on her mittens

and her warm tail sock.

She took off for Bo's.

Annie's feet sank deep

in the soft snow.

The moonlight made big shadows.

Annie did not like them.

But she wanted to find Bo.

She saw a scary shape.

It was coming right toward her.

There was no place

to hide.

Annie stopped.

The scary shape stopped, too.

"Annie?" it said.

Annie knew that voice.

"Bo!" she said. "Why are you

such a scary shape?"

"Because I have the surprise

on my head," said Bo.

"Oh, Bo!" said Annie.

"That is a very big surprise!"

She threw her arms around him.

"Ouff!" said Bo.

The surprise flew off his head.

CHAPTER 8

Bo and Annie stared at the surprise.

"What is it?" asked Annie.

"It *was* a full moon cake," said Bo.

"It *was* big and round and golden.

It *was* just like the moon.

Now look. It is a big mess."

Bo felt awful.

He threw himself down in the snow.

His tail sock flew off.

Snow got in his pants.

He felt worse.

"Wait, Bo!" said Annie.

"I have an idea.

Stay right here."

Annie ran off.

She came back with two forks.

"It used to be a full moon cake," she said.

"Now it is a snowy moon cake."

She handed Bo a fork.

"We better eat fast," he said.

"Or it will be a frozen moon cake."

Soon the cake was all gone.

They went back to Annie's house.

"Now I will make *you* a surprise," she said.

Annie ran upstairs.

Bo waited downstairs.

He was freezing cold.

He had snow in his pants.

He had snowy moon cake in his tummy.

Annie came back downstairs.

She had nothing in her hands.

She had nothing on her head.

"I don't see any surprise," said Bo.

"It's too big to carry," said Annie.

"Come with me."

Bo followed Annie upstairs.

"Surprise!" said Annie.

"A big hot bath. Just for you."

"YES!" said Bo.

And he jumped right in.